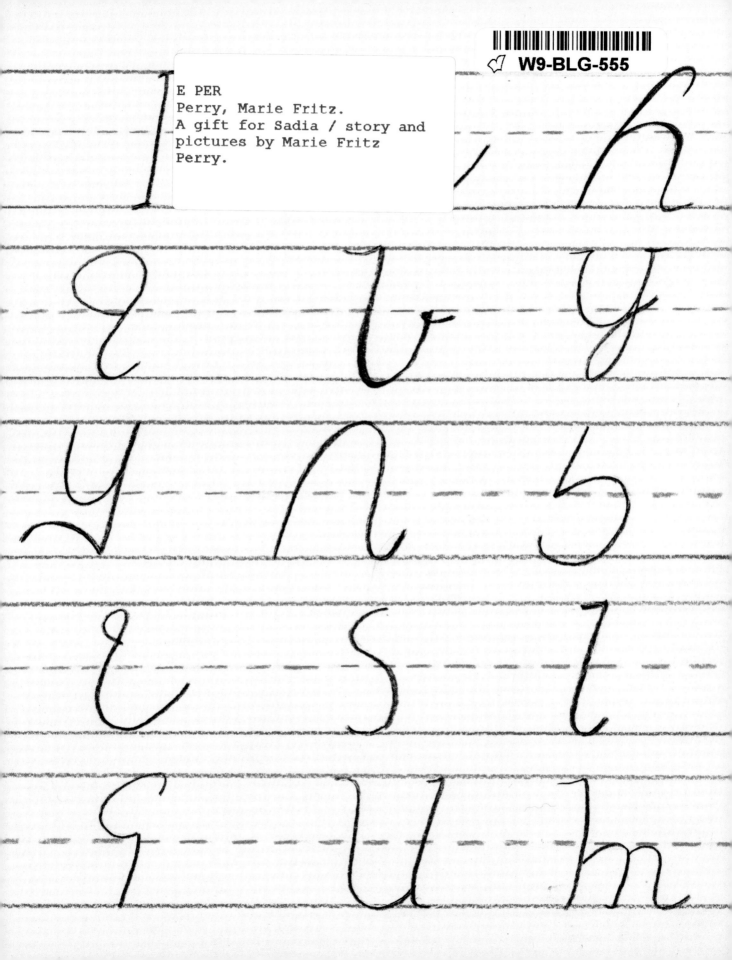

A GIFT FOR SADIA

story and pictures by MARIE FRITZ PERRY

Buttonweed Press, L.L.C.
Northfield, MN

Buttonweed Press, L.L.C.
7625 110th Street East
Northfield MN 55057
info@buttonweedpress.com

A Gift for Sadia

Printed in the United States by Northfield Printing, Inc. The illustrations in this book were executed in color pencil and pastel. The text of this book is set in 16 point Minion Pro. Layout is by Peter B. Nelson.

Publisher's Cataloging-in-Publication
(Provided by Quality Books, Inc.)

Perry, Marie Fritz.
  A gift for Sadia / written and illustrated by Marie Fritz Perry. — 1st ed. p. cm.
  SUMMARY: A young Somali girl immigrates to Minnesota and through the friendship of a wounded Canada goose learns how to accept her new life in America.
  Audience: Ages 5-9.
  ISBN 0-9755675-1-9
  LCCN 2004096209
  1. Somali Americans—Juvenile fiction. [1. Somali Americans—Fiction. 2. Immigrants—Fiction. 3. Canada
goose—Fiction. 4. Minnesota—Fiction.]   I. Title.

PZ7.P4354Gif 2004   [E]
QBI04-700503

Author's Note

At times, we all feel different or overwhelmed by change, so Sadia's story can touch all of us whether we have moved to another country or not. In 1998 I was lucky to meet a very special group of children who inspired this story. I worked as an artist-in-residence for the Rochester, Minnesota public school system teaching children's book illustration. My first day in the schools brought me a great surprise--I was informed by the principal of Hoover Elementary School that one group of children participating in the program did not speak English. These children had immigrated with their families from many parts of the world and were a part of the English-as-a-second-language (ESL) program.

My week-long project with these children taught me that they had plenty of their own stories to illustrate and we communicated with one another through our art. I was so inspired by what I saw and learned that I decided to arrange a special project with the ESL students enrolled in the Rochester Elementary Schools.

At Harriet Bishop Elementary school, I worked with the teachers to select seven ESL children representing Romania, Laos, Cambodia, Korea, Mexico and Somalia. With the help of their ESL teacher, the children wrote stories, drew pictures, and told me what they could about their experiences immigrating to the U.S. Despite their diverse backgrounds, a similar thread was being woven as I began to learn from them what it was like to start their lives over in a foreign nation and to learn in a foreign tongue. They all had so many similar obstacles to overcome even though they came from many different parts of the world, but one child stood out.

This particular student had immigrated from Somalia and although she wore western clothing, she kept to her religious values which required her to keep her hair covered. She had also left a war-torn nation with her family, and lived in a refugee camp located in Kenya for three years before relatives living in the U.S. were allowed to sponsor her family's immigration to the United States. Through her experience, I realized the importance of sharing what I learned from seven special children through a story that will hopefully make us all realize what it would be like to be an ESL student in America.

This book is for my father, Henry E. Fritz who gave me my love of animals and of other cultures and for my mother, Dolores M. Fritz who gave me my love of art.

A special thanks to Zeinab, Joe, Mellisa, Costin, Jairo, Kong, Hyeong-Min and the staff at Harriet Bishop Elementary in Rochester, Minnesota, as well as the staff and students of Sibley Elementary in Northfield, Minnesota. I would also like to thank East African (E.A.) Bilingual Services in St. Paul, Minnesota for their donation of time translating English into the Somali language for this book. I am also deeply thankful to my husband Jim and to my children Neil and Amalia for their help, love and support during this process!

A strange chill ran up Sadia's back as the tip of her finger touched the window pane above her new bed. The window was the coldest thing she could ever remember. Her finger touching the frosted glass made the frost disappear, leaving a tiny clear spot.

As Sadia peered through the opening, she looked out upon a very strange place. She could see a street with cars and just beyond was an area of frozen water with black and white birds all around it. "How cold these birds must be," thought Sadia. "How cold am I, too, in this new place they call Rochester!" she said aloud. Sadia could hear her mother telling her it was time for school, "Kaalay, cunugyahow, waa waqtigii iskuulka!" Sadia ran quickly to join her mother.

SILVER LAKE
PADDLEBOAT RIDES
CANOE RENTALS

The cold air brought tears to Sadia's eyes as she and her mother slipped and slid on the icy sidewalk leading to Sadia's new school.

The loud ringing bell frightened her. She wanted to tell someone, but her mother was the only one who could understand her language, Somali, and she was already leaving.

Instead, Sadia was led by a very tall man to a classroom filled with many children who looked different from her and each other. There were children from Laos, Korea, Cambodia, Mexico and Romania, and they were all placed together so that they could learn English.

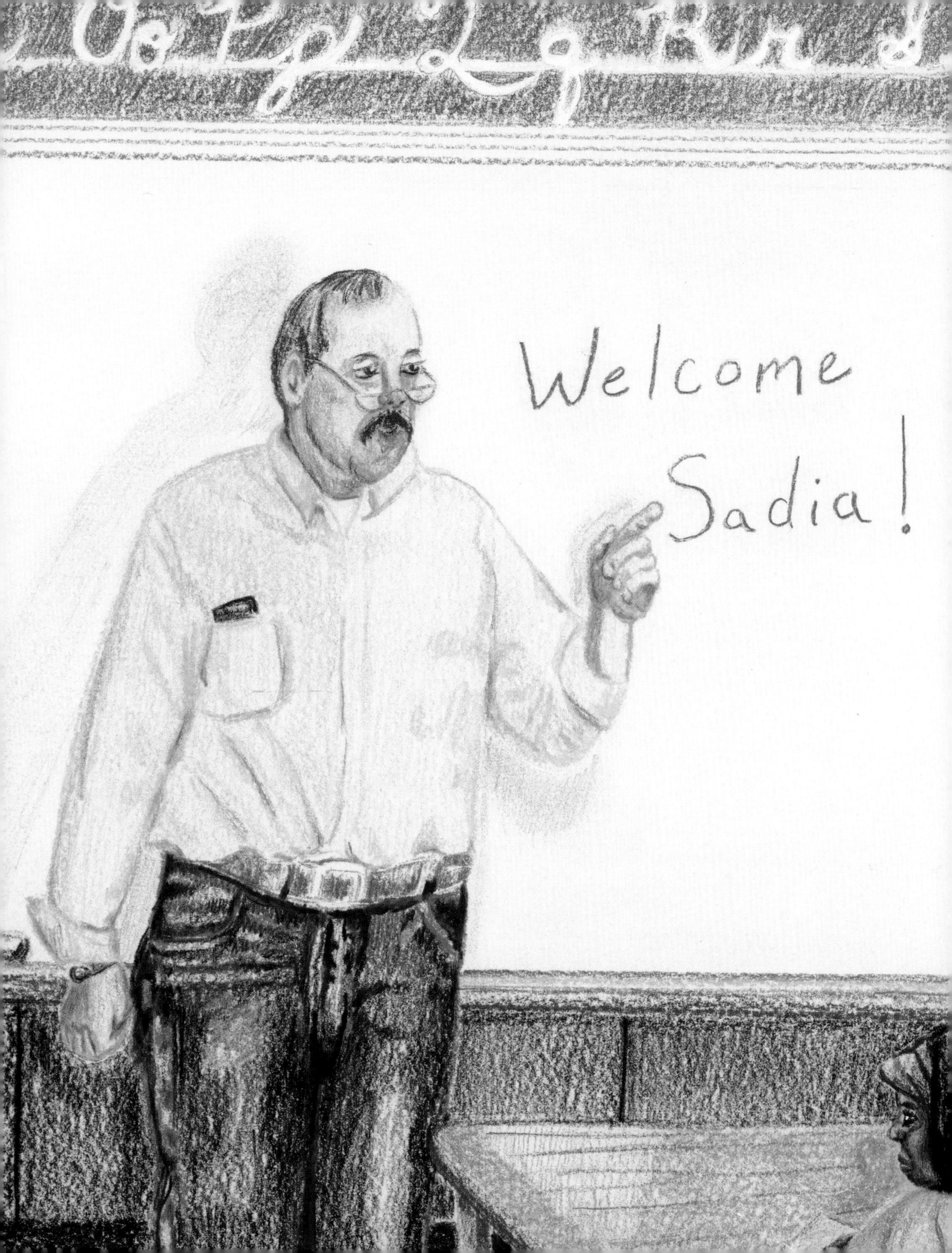
Welcome
Sadia!

The tall man, her teacher, began to speak to them in English introducing Sadia to the class. He then turned to her and said, "Today you will begin to learn your ABC's, Sadia." Sadia could not understand a word.

Sadia kept on going to school, but it wasn't like it had been in Somalia, "If only there hadn't been a war, then we could have stayed in Somalia. Mother said it was the war that made us come here!"

Sadia felt as cold inside as the air was outside. It was February now, the heart of winter in Minnesota. Sadia's only pleasure came from watching these strange black and white birds from her bedroom window. She noticed that people would come to feed them bread and corn, but there was one small bird, one with an injured wing, that could never get to the feast on time. The other stronger birds would quickly snap up the treats, leaving nothing for the wounded bird to eat.

Sadia showed her mother the bird, "She will go hungry and die if I do not feed her. May I share some of my dinner tonight with her, mother?" But her mother said, "I've been told by my cousin, who has lived here for many years, that these birds are called geese and they are very special to Rochester. They too come from another country, and the city has even put up vending machines for people to buy them food."

"It is we who will go hungry and die if we do not take care to eat our dinner. That bird does not need your help."

SILVER LAKE

Sadia sadly climbed the steps to her room again and cleared the frost from her window pane with her breath to get a better view.

There was the bird, the Canadian goose, sitting by herself again. She looked cold and lonely, the way Sadia felt. Sadia made up her mind to see that the bird was fed.

That evening, Sadia was lucky that her parents did not notice her sneak the crusts of her bread into her shirt sleeve. After dinner she excused herself and put on her warm clothes to go outside.

"Crack!" went the screen door as it slammed back against the frame, but Sadia was already across the street nearing the wounded goose.

Sitting alone underneath a large Scotch pine tree, the bird made no attempt to flee as Sadia knelt beside it. "Poor dear bird," Sadia thought to herself. "You need food to keep your spirits up. My mother tells me you and I have many more days in this cold place before the whispering warm winds from Somalia reach us."

The goose stretched its long winding neck out and nibbled the bread crusts from Sadia's open hand. A flutter of delight rustled all the way through its feathers, ending with a little wiggle from its tail. Sadia knew the bird was pleased. Choking back the tears, she said, "You understand me, don't you? It doesn't matter to you what language I speak."

And so it went for weeks with Sadia sneaking whatever leftovers she could manage to the bird. While the bird ate, Sadia would pour out her deepest sorrows. She told the bird about how the other children in her class had managed to learn the English alphabet, but it wasn't coming easily for her. Soon it would be time for her to recite the alphabet out loud to the class, and Sadia knew she would be too frightened to remember the correct order of the letters. Sadia comforted herself by watching her goose nibble the day's offerings.

Sadia crossed the blacktop of the school's playground on a warm
spring morning. The distant sounds of children's laughter and
motion of the swings
only reminded her
of how lonely
she felt.

As the bell rang, Sadia found herself caught in a sea of bodies all pushing through the narrow opening of the main door and into her classroom.

Sadia heard her name
called and she trembled.
Her classmates could feel her fear as she walked to the front
of the room. Her teacher said in his warmest voice, "Sadia, could you
please recite the alphabet for us?" Sadia stared at the floor. She could
not bear to look up at her classmates' faces. "A, B, C," she began
softly without raising her eyes. It wasn't until she reached the letter
"U" that she got stuck. "What comes next?" she mumbled to herself.

As tears touched her face, she heard the low honking sounds of geese. She looked up and out the window and saw that in the lead was her bird. Her classmates and teacher pointed and smiled at the geese. Seeing the V-formation in the sky, Sadia sputtered loudly "V," and then, "X, Y, Z." Sadia had cared for her goose through the cold winter months and now it was the goose's turn to look after her. This was the bird's gift to Sadia.

Cheers of delight rose up from her teacher and the other children in the room.

As Sadia looked out the window once more to see her goose returning to the lake, she knew she was finally home.

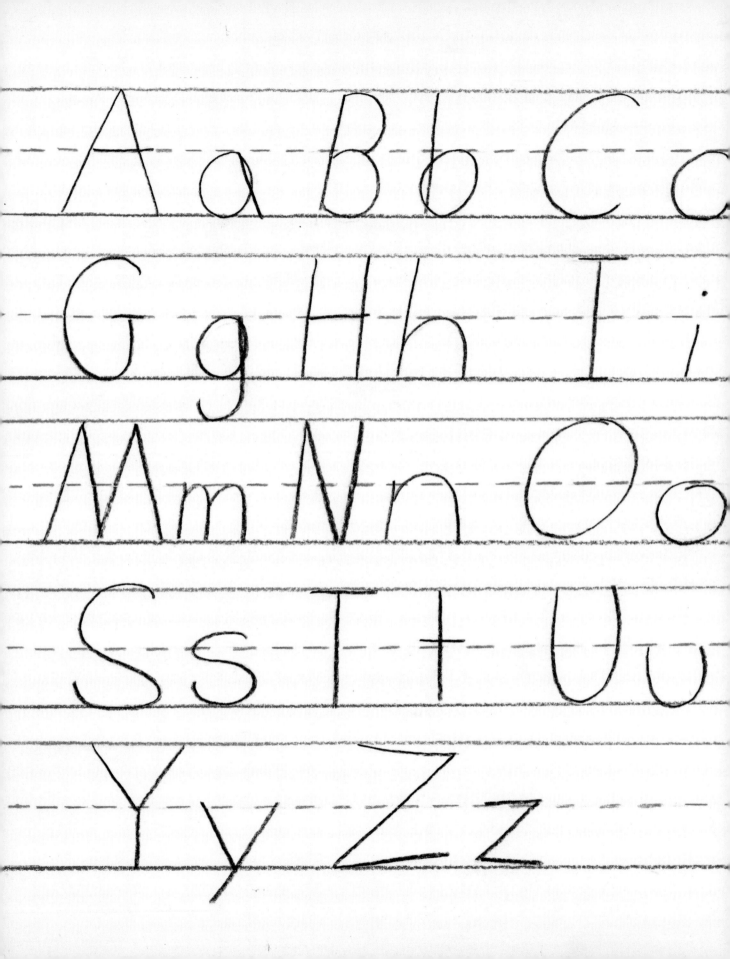